SCREWTOP THOMPSON

SCREWTOP THOMPSON

AND OTHER TALES

MAGNUS MILLS

B L O O M S B U R Y

LONDON • BERLIN • NEW YORK • SYDNEY

This edition published in Great Britain 2010

The first eight stories in this collection were originally published by Acorn Press*

Copyright © 2010 by Magnus Mills

The moral right of the author has been asserted

Bloomsbury Publishing Plc
36 Soho Square
London W1D 3QY

www.bloomsbury.com

Bloomsbury Publishing, London, New York and Berlin

A CIP catalogue record for this book is available from the British Library

ISBN 978 1 4088 0653 1

10 9 8 7 6 5 4 3 2 1

Typeset by Hewer Text UK Ltd, Edinburgh
Printed in Great Britain by Clays Limited, St Ives plc

* in collections entitled *Only When the Sun Shines
Brightly* and *Once in a Blue Moon*

For Special K

Contents

Only When the Sun Shines Brightly

For a long time I lived beside a railway viaduct that took the trains past my house at rooftop level. It was a brick structure almost a quarter of a mile in length, and ran along the far side of our street. This being a busy commercial district, the rail-freight company had at some date closed up the supporting arches and let them out as business premises. Some spaces were rented by wholesalers who used them for warehousing. Others had been converted into workshops. The one opposite me was presently occupied by a joiner called Nesbitt. It was a noisy place, with lathes and power-saws going at all hours of the day, augmented every now and then by the trains trundling overhead. A locomotive pulling a heavy load could make all the buildings vibrate as it went past, but fortunately the line was only used for shunting and therefore traffic was infrequent. To tell the truth, I quite liked all the coming and going. It was nice arriving home in the afternoon and seeing the joiner's shop in full swing, especially when Nesbitt had a big job under-way. On these occasions there would be staircases or window sashes leaning on the outside wall await-ing collection, while he and his two assistants busily prepared the next piece. One of these helpers was a youth who was supposed to be serving an appren-ticeship, but seemed actually to spend most of his time sweeping up wood shavings. The other was an old hand called Stanley. Nesbitt's business methods appeared at first glance chaotic, as he tended to write down his estimates on used envelopes which he then inevitably lost, but the fact that he always had plenty of work was testimony to his basic abilities. I used to go over to the workshop sometimes and have a cup of tea with the three of them. Most days, however, I just gave a cheery wave as I passed by.

Early one morning at the beginning of autumn I heard an odd sound coming from outside. At first I thought I'd been woken by the first shunter of the day, which generally went down the line at about five-thirty. This struck me as unusual because I'd become quite accustomed to all the din and could ordinarily sleep through anything. I lay listening for a few moments, and soon realised that it wasn't a train I'd heard. Instead, there came from the direction of the viaduct an irregular flapping noise, as of great wings being beaten. A bit of a breeze seemed to have got up during the night, which was nothing unusual at this time of year, and whenever a gust battered against my window the flapping became more noticeable. Yet for some reason I still couldn't think what might be causing it.

Eventually I decided it was time to get up, so I dressed and opened the blinds. It was barely daylight, but I couldn't help seeing an enormous plastic sheet caught up on the viaduct wall above Nesbitt's workshop. Somehow it had become entangled in the iron railing that ran along the top of the wall, and now hung outstretched in the breeze like some immense flag.

I wondered where on earth it could have come from. Pieces of debris quite often came flying in as the autumn equinox took hold, items such as polythene bin-liners and carrier bags, but never had anything as big as this arrived. It was a piece of industrial wrapping, possibly twenty square yards in area, and I assumed it must have come adrift from the back of some lorry or goods truck. All the same, it must have been a strong wind to lift such a large bit of flotsam into the air and carry it here. As I made myself a pot of tea I vaguely wondered what Nesbitt would have to say on the matter.

'It'll work itself free after a while,' he announced, as we stood looking up at the plastic sheet later that morning. 'Then we'll get hold of it and put it to some use.'

Nesbitt was forever talking about 'putting things to some use'. Quite often he could be observed peering into a builder's skip and pulling out some object that took his fancy; for example, a barrow that had been discarded because it had no wheel, or an empty cable drum. As a result, the corners of his workshop were piled with junk which he'd decided might come in handy at some future time. It appeared now that he'd seen a possible use for this huge plastic sheet, and as soon as he could get his hands on it, he would claim it for his own.

Unfortunately, getting his hands on it was more difficult than he foresaw. When I came home that afternoon the sheet had failed to free itself from the railings, and if anything seemed to have become fixed even more firmly than before. The weather had been deteriorating all day as the wind increased to a minor gale, and the flapping noise had grown louder and more insistent. Drawing near, I saw that Nesbitt now had a ladder against the viaduct wall, and had sent up his apprentice to seize the prize. The ladder, though, was nowhere near long enough for the task, and as the hapless youth poked desperately with a broom handle he looked as though he was going to lose his balance at any minute.

Nesbitt's other assistant, Stanley, had taken the opportunity to stop working and watch this bit of 'sport' from the workshop doorway, and as I approached he gave me a sidelong wink.

'He'll never get that down,' he murmured quietly. 'Not in a month of Sundays.'

'Why doesn't he go to the end of the viaduct and walk back along?' I suggested.

'It's railway property, isn't it?' he replied. 'No one's allowed up there.'

Meanwhile, Nesbitt was losing patience with his apprentice's efforts.

'Try and reach up a bit more!' he kept shouting, which only seemed to make the lad look even more unsteady.

'Notice he doesn't go up there himself?' remarked Stanley, before sidling back to his workbench.

'Come down then!' yelled Nesbitt, before turning to me. 'Useless, young lads are these days. Flaming useless.'

I thought for a moment that he was going to give his apprentice a clip round the ear for his troubles, but after he'd carefully descended they simply took down the ladder and put it away. Next thing Nesbitt and Co. were back at work on their latest joinery project, and appeared temporarily to have given up with the salvage attempt. Nonetheless, the presence of the plastic sheet was difficult to ignore. From inside my house I could hear a constant succession of flapping, whacking and flogging noises, and as the hours passed the racket worsened progressively. I knew, however, that I could do nothing about it, so I closed the blinds, put the kettle on, and had a cup of tea. Before coming in I'd noticed large drops of moisture in the gathering dusk. Soon afterwards it was raining cats and dogs, the drainpipes were flowing at full pelt, and I realised that autumn was now well and truly with us.

★

One of Aesop's fables tells the story of a wager between the sun and the wind to see which can succeed in removing a traveller's heavy coat. The wind tries first, but however hard it blows it fails to make any headway because the traveller simply buttons his coat even tighter than before. Only when the sun shines brightly does he finally remove it, and the wind roars away in a bad temper.

I was reminded of this fable several times over the next few days, as the wind seemed to be equally unsuccessful with our plastic sheet. It blew like fury for half a week, but the sheet remained firmly attached to the top of the viaduct. Occasionally it became trapped in the railings at more than one point, bellying out and filling with rainwater which would then be released at unexpected times over Nesbitt's doorway. At one such instance the poor fellow was standing directly underneath when it emptied its heavy load, drenching him from head to foot.

I soon noticed that Nesbitt had ceased to regard the plastic sheet as a 'lucky find', but instead glared up at it balefully for long moments as he tried to work out how to get it down. One afternoon I saw him trying to catch at it with a crude grappling hook on the end of a rope, assisted by Stanley and the young apprentice. Each of them tried and tried again to throw the hook up and get a grip, but they failed every time and had to move quickly out of the way as it came plummeting back down.

'Why don't you write to the rail company?' I suggested. 'They'll be able to get at it easily.'

'Yes, you're right,' replied Nesbitt. 'I think I will.'

However, I knew for a fact that he wouldn't. Nesbitt wasn't the kind of man to spend time writing letters to railway companies. He had a business to run on a day-to-day basis, and the plastic sheet was really nothing more than an irritating diversion. He would repeatedly claim to be 'doing something about it', but his efforts amounted to nothing more than vain assaults with a grappling hook. Meanwhile, I suspected that Stanley found the whole episode thoroughly entertaining. As for me, well I was beginning slowly to get used to the plastic sheet. I would fall asleep at night to the sound of it whacking and flapping against the viaduct wall, and wake up in the morning to the same thing. It was rapidly becoming part of the scenery, the first object I laid eyes on when I opened my blinds, and I soon learned to live with it. Whenever friends arrived at my front door they would pass comment on the 'eyesore' dangling from the viaduct, suggesting that it lowered the tone of the neighbourhood. I countered such remarks by pointing at all the everyday litter blowing along the street.

'We live in an untidy world,' I would declare in a glib sort of way. 'You've got to expect a certain amount of industrial detritus in a district like this.'

Judging by the looks on their faces, my friends seemed to find my argument spurious, to say the least.

★

One blustery day a month or so later, a small diesel locomotive chugged slowly along the railway viaduct, paused above Nesbitt's workshop, and then continued on its way. A minute later it came reversing back to where the plastic sheet still lay trapped. A door in the driver's cab slid open, and three men climbed out, all wearing orange fluorescent jackets. They peered over the railing at the sheet as it flogged in the damp breeze, and then began disentangling it. After a while Nesbitt emerged and stood in the street offering words of encouragement. At least, that was what they sounded like from where I watched at my window. It took the three men almost ten minutes to gather the sheet in and fold it up. Then, when they'd exchanged greetings with Nesbitt, they climbed back into their cab and moved off, taking the plastic sheet with them.

That night our street seemed very quiet indeed, and it took me a long time to get to sleep.

At Your Service

My friend Mr Wee was only five feet tall, so if he ever had any domestic chores that required a bit more 'height' I used to go round and help out. If I was lucky he cooked me Chinese food as a reward. If not (which was more often the case) I got tea and burnt toast. Mr Wee's manner was imperious to say the least, but in spite of this the pair of us generally got on very well together.

One day he summoned me to his flat and ordered me to bring my bowsaw.

'There is a tree obscuring my view,' he told me.

I arrived on Sunday morning and removed my boots (a prerequisite for entry into the Wee household on account of his spotless carpets). Then I knocked and waited. There was no answer. I knocked again, and after another minute the door opened. Mr Wee examined my feet and ushered me inside without apologising for the delay.

'I was just bathing the cats.'

As we passed through the hallway I saw his two cats glaring at me from the bathroom, their Sunday morning treat having been temporarily interrupted. They were yet to be rinsed, so I continued my wait in the lounge. The gramophone played Beethoven, and on the shelves stood marble busts of all the great composers. They watched in silence as I awaited the return of Mr Wee. Eventually the ablutions were completed and he came back, sat down and lit his pipe.

The tree in question was outside the rear window (Mr Wee lived on the second floor). It was a great overgrown thorny thing, and he expected me to climb into it and remove some branches. I asked if we were allowed to do this.

'Of course,' he snapped with a note of impatience. 'I've spoken to the property manager.'

'We'll need a ladder,' I said.

'Of course.'

Apparently it was all arranged: we were to carry the (borrowed) ladder through a ground-floor flat belonging to one of Mr Wee's neighbours. I wasn't sure if I liked the sound of this, but decided to say nothing. I got my boots back on and we collected the ladder. Then we went to the other flat.

'Shall I take my boots off again?' I asked.

'No,' he replied. 'She won't mind.'

He knocked on the door and it was opened by an elderly lady. This was Mrs Petrov.

'We're coming through with the ladder,' announced Mr Wee.

'But it's Sunday morning,' she protested, in a strong Polish accent.

He ignored her and bustled into the flat, taking the ladder with him. Mrs Petrov followed and closed the door. I remained outside, waiting. Presently I heard raised voices within. Suddenly the door was flung open and Mrs Petrov commanded me to come and help immediately. I dashed into the flat and found Mr Wee disentangling the ladder from her kitchen curtains. She began shouting at him. He shouted back at her. Then she noticed my boots and shouted at me. Quickly I got the ladder out through the back door.

Some moments later Mr Wee emerged and the two of us started to examine the tree. I remarked that it was going to be a bit of a balancing act and I was likely to get thorns stuck in me. This did not concern him.

'Are you afraid of heights?' he asked.

I said I was not, and started up the ladder. As I did so I noticed curtains beginning to twitch in another of the flats. Feeling very uneasy I continued climbing. Then a man appeared looking rather upset.

'What are you doing?' he demanded of Mr Wee.

'This tree is obscuring my view,' came the reply.

'But you're treading all over my garden!'

Mr Wee looked down at some crushed flowers beneath his feet. He muttered something and led the poor fellow away. I stayed in the tree.

Hearing no more raised voices I commenced work, choosing the largest branch that could be safely removed with a bowsaw. After much sweat and toil, it dropped neatly to the ground.

Mr Wee came back and peered up into the foliage.

'Not that branch, *that* one!' he roared, pointing to a large and almost vertical bough.

'I can't cut that!' I yelled back. 'I'll probably kill myself or put it through someone's window!'

Mr Wee stamped round in a fury while I sawed away at a few other branches until we'd both calmed down a bit. Then I descended. He looked at the finished job and said he 'supposed' that would have to do.

Running the gauntlet of Mrs Petrov again, we returned to his flat. I pointed out that his view was no longer obstructed. In fact, so much light was flooding into the room that Mr Wee decided to close the curtains, thus defeating the object of the exercise.

He grudgingly offered to make me a cup of tea for my troubles, but on this occasion there was to be no Chinese food.

The Comforter

I was looking for a way into the cathedral when the archdeacon found me. There were several doors, and I had paused before one of them.

'Locked, is it?' he asked, smiling.

'Well, I haven't actually . . . er . . . not sure really.'

'Probably locked,' he announced. 'Probably far too early. I always arrive far too early.'

The archdeacon laughed in a beneficent way and I smiled.

'You must be the architect,' he beamed.

'I suppose I am,' I replied. 'Yes.'

'Very good. Very pleased you could come. There's a door along here we can try.'

He shepherded me round the corner, past some shrubs and newly emerging bulbs. On this side of the building it was damp and shady, and there was a smaller door. It was locked.

'They're trying to keep us out, I think!' he laughed again. This time it was a compulsory laugh, and I joined in. The archdeacon's face was pink, his eyes were blue, his hair was white. He smiled a lot and took me under his wing. We sat down, side by side, on a wooden bench.

'They always seem to rope me in for these committees,' said the archdeacon, placing his briefcase flat across his knees. 'Probably think it'll keep me out of mischief! They're most probably right!' This time I anticipated the laughter, which seemed to please him.

'Would you like a sandwich?' he asked, opening the lid. 'I'm supposed to keep papers in here, but to tell you the truth I hardly ever get round to reading them. Always get given lots of papers. In case I miss something, I suppose. Good job really. My wife says I never listen. Not properly. Still, it all goes down in the minutes. I'm just there to agree with everyone really. Salmon and cucumber, I think. Yes. Like one?'

I said, 'Thank you, no,' and he turned and smiled with bushy eyebrows raised.

'You don't mind if I . . . ?'

'No, no. Of course not. Bon appétit.'

'Ah, merci.'

The swallows were skimming low and it might rain soon. I could feel the dampness coming through from the bench, but it would have been rude of me to rise. So I waited while the archdeacon broke his bread alone. Silence had fallen, for the moment, on our small corner of the world. One of the flagstones between the bench and the door had a crack across it, from which moss grew. Some of the others had signs of weakness, here and there. I began to count them, from left to right, in my head, but the silence had become too much for my companion.

'Lovely garden, don't you think?'

'Yes.'

'Absolutely lovely. Abounds with flowers in summer. There's a man comes from the council, twice a week. Sort of loan, I believe. Do you know him?'

'I'm afraid not.'

'Very nice man. Will always give you the time of day. Very nice. Always sweeps up.'

'That's good,' I said.

'Yes indeed.'

We smiled and nodded together. A moment passed.

'Cost a lot, will it?' he asked. 'This new roof?'

'I'm not sure.'

'Can't be helped, I suppose. Nothing lasts forever.'

I glanced at my watch.

'Oh dear,' said the archdeacon, closing his lid and rising quickly. 'Rather damp, this bench.'

Here was the opportunity for me to rise as well, and we paced about upon the flagstones, turning our backs on the breeze that was getting up. The shrubs rustled as the archdeacon fastened his overcoat buttons, an empty briefcase clamped between his knees. In the tower high above a bell struck nine.

'This always happens to me when I arrive early somewhere,' he said, preparing to see the funny side of it. 'I end up being late.'

We waited.

'Aren't there any others?' I asked.

'Should be,' he replied. 'Usually seven or eight at least.'

'Perhaps we should try the front door again.'

'Wasn't it locked?'

'Well, I thought you said it was.'

He pulled a face. 'Oh dear.'

★

The front door was not locked, but because of the archdeacon, we entered the cathedral late. The rest of the committee were waiting inside, still wearing their coats.

'So sorry,' he explained. 'Slight misunderstanding about which door.'

His arrival brought in the fresh air from outside. They forgave him with a shiver.

'Better late than never, Norman,' said the chairman, leading the way to where an antechamber had been prepared. There was a round table surrounded by wooden chairs with leather seats, and in the corner stood a cylinder-gas heater, pale flames flickering on the gauze. As we looked for our places the archdeacon took command.

'Now I'm going to sit next to you because I know absolutely nothing about architecture!'

He sat down in the treasurer's seat beside mine, in spite of the card marked 'Treasurer'. The chairman's table plan was now upset. He tried to intervene. The archdeacon did not listen. He was telling me about his pen.

'Gift from the last chancellor. Christmas 1972 it was. No, sorry, '71. Very nice man. Always exchanged gifts at Christmas. Without fail. Terrible loss and we miss him greatly. Never let me down, this pen.' He removed its cap, examined the nib and then replaced the cap again.

'Won't be needing it today, of course. Not with all these pencils Frank provides. Always a box of pencils. You wouldn't believe it. If I had all the pencils . . . oh, we're ready, are we, Frank? Sorry.'

★

The chairman, meanwhile, had made diplomatic moves and managed to rearrange the table plan without the archdeacon even noticing. At last we were all seated and the minutes of the previous meeting were read aloud.

Beside me the archdeacon had fallen silent for the time being. As business proceeded and various points were raised, he carefully balanced his pencil at the edge of his pad. If he placed a finger on one end of the pencil, it would dip and touch the table surface. When he removed his finger it became level again. After half an hour he suddenly took up his pencil and wrote LIGHT BULB in block letters across one corner of the pad. The rest of the time he nodded and smiled, and gave the appearance of listening.

At the end of the first session, the chairman addressed the archdeacon: 'Unless you've got anything to add to that, Norman?'

'No, no,' said my neighbour with confidence. 'Sounds fine to me.'

There then followed a welcome break for coffee and biscuits. Before I had a chance to stretch myself, a firm hand took me by the arm and led me over to a newly opened hatch.

As he offered a plate of Malted Milks the archdeacon spoke in a low voice. 'Not going too bad, is it?'

'So far, no,' I agreed.

'Not too bad at all. Odd that they haven't mentioned the roof yet.'

'Odd?'

'Yes. Must be a trial for your patience.'

'Why's that?'

'You being the architect and everything.' He looked at me. 'You did say you were the architect, didn't you?'

'Yes, architect would be one way of describing me,' I replied. 'I sort of plan things really. Set things up.'

'Oh,' he said. 'I see.'

The archdeacon stirred sugar into his coffee before he spoke again. 'But we will be getting onto the roof eventually, won't we?' he asked.

'Eventually,' I said.

When we got back to the committee table the chairman had already been round tidying up. The archdeacon's pencil, for example, had been returned to the holder in the centre of the table. Also the place cards indicating people's status had been rearranged in the new order dictated by the archdeacon's decision to sit next to me. As I resumed my seat I selected a pencil for the second session, and chose one for the archdeacon too.

'How kind,' he remarked, preparing to balance it again at the edge of his pad.

The second session continued in much the same way as the first, with a number of reports being read out and approved. After a while the archdeacon drew a circle around LIGHT BULB, the outline of which he renewed from time to time as the hours passed, until it became a dark ring surrounding the words. Then he added a pair of ears at the top of the circle, as well as some cats' whiskers, before laying his pencil down.

The gas-cylinder heater in the corner had taken the earlier coolness out of the room, and now, humming quietly, it began to devour the remaining fresh air. There were no windows that could be opened for ventilation, and because the walls were thick, few sounds came in from the world outside. Apart from the hourly chiming of the bell in the tower above, the discussions of the committee were all that could be heard.

At one o'clock the chairman announced that it was time for lunch, and the archdeacon immediately got up and headed for the door.

'Where are you going, Norman?' asked the chairman.

'Just a little errand I've got to run,' replied the archdeacon. 'Won't be long.'

'But we're having a working lunch. There isn't time for you to go wandering off anywhere.'

The archdeacon looked dismayed. 'I haven't any sandwiches left.'

'You can share mine,' I said.

'Oh,' said the archdeacon, returning to his place. 'Thank you. You're so very kind.'

The other members of the committee all had packed lunches wrapped in silver foil. Some also had apples, while some had individual fruit pies or cakes. My sandwiches were plain Cheddar cheese, but there were enough for two.

The archdeacon ate in silence as further conversation was exchanged around the table. Then, before the afternoon session began in earnest, he was permitted a brief stroll around the cathedral close, just to stretch his legs. I offered to accompany him and we went outside.

'I must say,' he confided, as the door swung shut behind us, 'I've never attended such a long meeting before. Seems to be going on forever.'

'Well, there's a lot to cover,' I said.

'Oh yes,' he replied. 'Yes, I can see that. Not that I'm complaining, of course. It's all very interesting.'

'Glad to hear it.'

The sky was dark. It had been raining. Our walk took us across wet flagstones and past the bench where we had sat that morning. We stopped to admire a hydrangea bush about to come into leaf. I glanced at my watch. We went back inside.

At two o'clock we took our seats again, and now some papers were circulated. The archdeacon played a helpful role here, passing the numbered pages around in their correct order, and placing his own in a neat pile before him. It seemed important to him that the corners of the pages should all be exactly lined up with each other, and he spent some considerable time ensuring this was so. After that, there was nothing else for him to do but sit and listen. If his opinion on some issue was asked, he would agree wholeheartedly with the previous speaker, but most of the time he was left to his own devices. Due to the gas-cylinder heater, the air in the room had now become thick and heavy, and the archdeacon was unable to prevent his eyes from occasionally closing. Every now and then I would notice his head nodding slowly forward as he drifted almost to the verge of sleep. Yet he never fully succumbed, and the tap of a pencil or a slight change in the speaker's tone of voice would be enough to snap his eyes wide open again. In this way the afternoon ticked past and gradually gave way to evening. Finally the bell in the tower above struck six and the meeting came to a close.

As the chairman gathered up some papers he looked over the rim of his glasses at the yawning archdeacon.

'Now don't forget, Norman. Bright and early tomorrow morning,' he said.

A puzzled look crossed the archdeacon's face.

'Tomorrow?' he asked.

'Of course,' replied the chairman.

'But I had no idea we were meeting tomorrow.'

The room had become very quiet.

'You're not trying to wriggle out of this, are you?'

'Well, no,' said the archdeacon, in an uncertain voice. 'But I thought it was only supposed to be twice a week. That's how it's always been. Tuesdays and Thursdays.'

The chairman rose from his seat and regarded the archdeacon. 'Tuesdays and Thursdays are no longer enough,' he announced. 'You'll be expected to come in tomorrow, and the next day, and every day after that. There can be no backing out now. It was all agreed at the last meeting.'

'Oh dear,' said the archdeacon, bowing his head. 'I can't have been listening properly.'

The chairman looked at me and nodded slowly. I placed my arm around the archdeacon's shoulder to offer some comfort.

'But that's always been your trouble, hasn't it, Norman?' I said. 'You never listen. Not properly.'

Hark the Herald

The narrow stairway had a wooden banister on each side, and was carpeted in red. I came down five steps, turned at a small landing, and stopped to examine a barometer on the wall. There were five more steps below me. He was waiting at the bottom.

'Morning, sir,' he said. 'Did you manage to get a good night's sleep?'

'Oh, morning,' I replied. 'Er . . . not quite, actually.'

'I'm very sorry to hear that, sir. Any particular reason?'

'Well, it's just that the merrymaking seemed to go on for a bit too long.'

'Merrymaking, sir?'

'Yes.'

'What sort of merrymaking?'

'I could hear all this laughing and singing. It kept me awake.'

'That's very odd, sir,' he said. 'None of the other guests have mentioned it.'

'Oh . . . haven't they?'

'No, they haven't. There's been no one complaining about any "merrymaking".'

'Oh no, I'm not complaining,' I said quickly. 'It's just that I thought it went on a bit too long, that's all.'

His name was Mr Sedgefield. I'd met him late the previous evening when I first arrived, and he had put me in their 'best single room'. Now he gave me a long, thoughtful look before speaking again.

'Well we don't want your Christmas spoilt, sir, so we'll have to look into the matter.'

'Thanks.'

He remained at the foot of the stairs gazing up at me, and for the first time I noticed he was wearing a kitchen apron emblazoned with a smiling pink pig. I felt unable to continue my descent until he'd moved out of the way, but he showed no inclination to do this so I turned my attention once again to the barometer.

'I see the pressure's fallen overnight.'

'Yes,' he said. 'Should make for some very interesting seas during the next day or two.'

'That's what I was thinking. Might be nice to have a stroll along the clifftops later.'

'If only we'd known your plans earlier, sir. You could have gone with the others. A whole party of them left not half an hour ago.'

'What, without breakfast?'

'Oh no, we made sure they all had breakfast first.'

'Does that mean I'm too late?'

'Of course not,' he said, stepping back at last and indicating the dining room. 'You might have missed the bacon and eggs, but we can always rustle up some porridge.'

I heard myself thanking him once again, and then continued my way downstairs. A large upright clock in the hall showed that it was five past nine. This didn't strike me as an unduly late time to be coming down for breakfast in a guest house, but it was obvious that everyone else had already been and gone. All the tables in the dining room were bare apart from a small one in the corner by the window. This had cup, saucer and cutlery set for one.

Mr Sedgefield ushered me towards it and I sat down just as another man appeared in the doorway and said, 'Sugar, honey or treacle?'

'Pardon?' I asked.

'In your porridge.'

'Oh, sorry. Er . . . treacle, please, if you've got it.'

This second man also wore a kitchen apron, but his depicted a laughing cow rather than a smiling pig.

'Righto,' he said, and next moment was gone again.

'Years since I've had porridge with treacle in it,' I remarked to Mr Sedgefield.

'Yes,' he replied. 'We have things here you can't often get in other parts of the country.'

'Actually, I didn't mean . . .' I began, but now he too had left the dining room.

In the last few moments he'd discreetly placed a small coffee pot on the table, so I poured myself a cup and took the opportunity to glance at my surroundings. The walls were arrayed with paintings and framed photographs of maritime scenes, past and present. In one picture an ocean liner with red funnels departed from some great international port. In the next, a fishing smack unloaded at the quay. There were yachts in black-and-white 'going to windward off Portland Bill', and others in colour with their spinnakers billowing. Meanwhile, ancient triremes prepared for battle in the Aegean. The nautical decor had been made festive with berries and seasonal greenery, but it was overdone somewhat, so that the Victory at Trafalgar now lay partially obscured by sprigs of holly. I'd seen the same sort of thing in the hallway when I arrived. Every attempt had been made to give the place a 'yuletide' feel, but behind the mistletoe and the tinsel there were always icebergs and distant lightships. It was the coastal setting that did it. This was a seaside guest house that catered mainly for summer visitors, and it was decked out according to their expectations.

Yet the place had its attractions in mid-winter too, which was why I'd decided to spend Christmas here. Through the window I could see a silver gleam where the sky and the sea reflected one another. A perfect place for getting the New Year off to an optimistic start.

The house stood on the clifftops above a cove. It had been built to withstand the extremities of weather, and although there were two storeys it was very squat and low. Hence the staircase with only ten steps. The rooms were small, and staying here somehow reminded me of being on board a ship. I'd arrived late the night before, when the place was in darkness. Mr Sedgefield had let me in and attended to everything, but I had been aware of someone else's presence in the kitchen at the end of the hall. Presumably this was the man who'd asked me about my porridge. We'd had a bit of a chat about the weather, during which I'd learnt that we were 'too far west' to get any snow in 'normal years'. Then I was given a mince pie and a glass of sherry before going up to bed.

I had hoped to be lulled straight to sleep by the sound of waves gently breaking on the seashore. Instead, I'd been kept awake for some time by all this laughing and singing. I couldn't tell what part of the house it was coming from, but it seemed to continue until the early hours. There were glasses tinkling as well.

Now I had no objection to people enjoying themselves. After all, it was Christmas, the season of goodwill, and they were only having a little harmless fun. I just thought it went on for a bit too long really, so I resolved to mention it to Mr Sedgefield when I saw him in the morning. Finally, the merrymaking ceased and I slept at last, but I was so exhausted that I failed to wake until almost nine o'clock, and there was only porridge left for breakfast.

★

The treacle had been poured over the top, but I was allowed to stir it in myself. Meanwhile, Mr Sedgefield hovered around the dining room and ensured that my coffee cup was replenished frequently. I had to admit that the service was excellent, although he did tend to fuss a little.

After a while he said, 'Don't mind me asking, sir, but did you have any plans for this evening?'

'Not really,' I answered.

'Well, if you're interested, some of the other guests are having a bit of a Christmas get-together later on.'

'Oh right.'

'There'll be games like snakes-and-ladders, charades and blind man's buff, as well as mince pies for everyone.'

'Sounds like fun.'

'Yes, indeed,' he said. 'And I'm sure they'd love you to join them.'

'Well, yes,' I replied. 'I'd be very glad to.'

'After supper then, in the reception room?'

'Right, I'll be there.'

'Good.' A moment passed, and then he asked, 'Porridge, alright, was it?'

'Delicious, thanks,' I said.

'It's a shame you had to miss the full breakfast, but of course you will be entitled to a packed lunch.'

'When?'

'When you go out.'

'Oh . . . er, OK, thanks.'

'You will be going out, won't you, sir?'

'Well, I hadn't definitely decided, but, yes, I expect I most probably will.'

'There are some fine walks to be had on the cliffs,' he announced. 'And if you're feeling particularly robust, I can strongly recommend the view at Temple Point.'

I wasn't feeling 'particularly robust' after my sleepless night, but it was clear that my host wanted me out for the day. Presumably this was so preparations could be made for the coming evening, and therefore I obliged him by agreeing that I would indeed be going for a walk later. Next thing he'd produced a map, which he opened and spread before me on the table.

'With a bit of luck you'll meet the other guests somewhere en route,' he said. 'I gather they're heading in the same direction.'

Temple Point turned out to be a spit of land protruding into the sea about four miles away to the west. Obviously Mr Sedgefield had more in mind for me than a casual seaside stroll, but by the time he'd indicated the waymarked paths and other suggested viewpoints I'd come fully to accept the idea. Besides, I thought, it would give me a good appetite for supper.

An hour later I was in the hallway putting on my boots when he emerged from the kitchen.

'We're just doing your sandwiches now, sir. Cheese be all right, will it?'

'Yes, fine, thanks.'

'Like an apple as well?'

'Please.'

'Right you are.'

He disappeared again, and for the next few moments I heard lowered voices speaking in the kitchen. Not wanting to eavesdrop on their conversation I stepped out into the porch, closing the front door behind me. In the corner stood a large Christmas tree. It was decorated with fairy lights, and as I waited I noticed them flicker a couple of times. Thinking there must be a loose bulb somewhere I began working round the tree, testing each one. I'd got about halfway when the door opened and Mr Sedgefield came out.

'Something wrong, sir?' he asked.

'Well,' I replied. 'There seems to be a fault somewhere. I was just looking for it.'

'Now don't you go worrying about that,' he said. 'You're supposed to be on holiday so just let me deal with any problems.'

'Oh . . . OK then.'

'Here you are.' He handed me a neat package in a greaseproof-paper bag. The clock in the hallway struck eleven. It was time for me to go.

'By the way,' I asked. 'What time's supper?'

'Whenever you like, sir,' he replied. 'Just take as long as you wish.'

★

The guest house was bounded on one side by a garden with ornamental trees and shrubs, including several rhododendrons. Behind it towards the sea lay open countryside, small fields with sparse hedges that gave out to tracts of bracken near the edge of the cliffs. I found the waymarked path and headed west.

The weather was mild but, because of the overnight drop in pressure, decidedly blustery. It also accounted for the 'interesting seas' that Mr Sedgefield had mentioned. The whole ocean seemed to be mounting a headlong charge against this stretch of the coast, with huge breakers crashing against the cliffs below. Not that I was complaining, of course. It was just this sort of wild bleakness that I'd come looking for. I walked with my head down into the wind, stopping from time to time to watch seabirds performing acrobatics above the waves. In one of the fields some cows stood huddled with their backs to the sea, nudging at a bale of hay that had been laid out for them. Here and there in the distance I could see occasional low buildings, some of which I took to be farmhouses, others I supposed were holiday homes to rent. What I didn't see, though, were people. No one else had chosen to walk the coastal path today, and there was no sign of Mr Sedgefield's other guests. Maybe they'd gone in the opposite direction.

It was mid-afternoon when I finally arrived at Temple Point. Here the cliffs had broken away to leave a great towering arch of rock, pounded on all sides by the white swirling waters and resembling some great piece of Gothic architecture. I clambered right to the end of the promontory, and then sat looking across at the arch. Every now and then a shower of spray would rise up from below, moment-arily threatening to engulf me before subsiding again. Meanwhile the soaring columns of rock stood immobile and unmoved by the surging waves. It was a marvellous sight.

I spent quite a while gazing out and pondering what primeval forces had conspired together to create such a place. Than I ate my sandwiches.

★

Darkness had fallen by the time I arrived back at the guest house, but surprisingly there was no sign of activity inside. This came as a bit of a disappointment. The walk home from Temple Point had seemed to take much longer than the outward journey, with the threat of rain coming in later, and I'd begun to look forward to a little Christmas cheer.

The get-together that Mr Sedgefield had spoken of now appeared most attractive. I could just imagine him and his partner fussing around in the reception room, lighting a log fire and preparing some fine mulled wine. Or perhaps roasting chestnuts. It would also be a chance at last to meet the other guests.

As it was, I came up the garden path to find the place silent and gloomy. Even the fairy lights in the porch had given up flickering and seemed finally to have gone out altogether. Before going inside I decided to complete my test on the bulbs. There were half a dozen left to do, and when I got to the last one I discovered it was loose.

I gave it the necessary twist and all the lights were restored.

Then I knocked on the door and waited.

A minute passed before Mr Sedgefield opened up.

'Ah,' he said. He was no longer wearing his apron.

'Ah,' I replied with a grin. 'I'm back.'

'Yes.'

I was led inside and we stood for a few awkward moments in the hall.

'Not too late for supper, am I?' As I spoke I real-ised my appetite had returned with a vengeance. I felt quite hungry again.

'Well,' he said. 'I suppose we could do you a cold plate at a push.'

'Is that what the others are having?'

'The others had theirs hours ago.'

'Oh . . . did they?'

'Indeed they did, and I'm sorry to say you've missed them again.'

'How?'

'They've gone carol-singing. Shame really, you could have gone with them.'

'But what about the get-together?'

'I'm afraid that's postponed.'

He showed me into the reception room, and then went off to the kitchen. There were no logs burning in the grate, only an electric fire with one bar switched on. And there were no decorations. When Mr Sedgefield finally returned he brought a plate with some cold pork, a few slices of bread and butter, and some pickle.

'Bon appétit,' he said.

I watched as he went to the dresser and opened a sherry bottle, pouring out three glasses. He gave one to me, and then carried the other two out of the room. He didn't come back.

The evening passed very slowly. I finished my supper and spent a while looking at some *National Geographic* magazines. There was enough sherry left in the bottle for another glass or two, but I was unwilling to help myself without asking. So at about half past ten I went up to my room.

I sat on the bed and listened. At any moment I hoped to hear the sound of merrymakers returning, followed soon afterwards by glasses tinkling and joyous voices calling me down to be with them.

Yet all I heard was the murmuring sea as it broke against the shore.

Once in a Blue Moon

My mother's house was under siege. One chill Friday evening in November I arrived to find the entire neighbourhood in a state of high alert. The police had blocked the street at both ends. A helicopter was circling overhead, and there were snipers hidden in the garden.

'Get down!' they hissed, when I approached.

'It's OK,' I replied. 'I've been on this case right from the beginning.'

After a couple of routine questions they directed me to the officer in command. He was a harassed-looking individual, sheltering with the rest of his men behind an armoured car. The guys were at a complete loss as to what to do next. They stood around, drinking coffee from paper cups, and waiting for something to happen. When I joined them I received no more than a cursory glance.

'Would you like me to talk to her?' I offered.

'Be my guest,' said the chief. 'When all this is over I'm handing in my badge. After that I'll be back on traffic duties. For good.'

He got on his radio and ordered the helicopter to move away. Then I ducked beneath a chequered tape bearing the words POLICE LINE: DO NOT CROSS.

To tell the truth I had scant idea what to expect. It was a while since I'd last called on my mother, having been fully occupied with work and so forth. The usual story. There was no excuse for my neglect, and as I crossed the garden towards the darkened dwelling I felt more than a little uneasy. A heavy silence lay about the place. The only disturbance was the humming of the power generators somewhere behind me. In the cold autumn air I could feel the heat of the searchlights on the back of my neck. There was nowhere to hide.

The commander had given me a loud-hailer. Now I raised it to my lips, spoke into the mouth-piece, and heard a staccato voice ricochet through the night.

'Alright, Mother!' it rasped. 'I'm going to count to three, and then I want you to come outside with your hands held high above your head.'

I lowered the loud-hailer and waited. From the house there came not a sound. Its blank windows seemed to stare down at me as I stood all alone in my mother's garden. I tried again.

'Can you hear me, Mother?!'

To the rear of me I could sense growing rest-lessness. I knew it wouldn't be too long before the police became impatient and began to resort to less subtle methods. This was my last chance.

'Mother?'

The quiet was shattered as an upper window exploded into smithereens. Then the barrel of a gun appeared, and behind it, my mother's face.

'Whaddyawant?!' she hollered.

It was a good question, and I realised I needed to think carefully before I answered. What I really wanted, of course, was to be able to converse with my mother as I had done in the past. Countless times the two of us had sat in her living room, exchanging remarks about the weather while we shared tea and buns. The clock on the shelf would tick resolutely round for half an hour or so, and then I'd take my

47

leave and all would be well. Her tone this evening, however, suggested that circumstances had changed. I was in danger of being viewed as a representative of the besieging forces. Therefore I required an angle.

'We were wondering,' I said, addressing her once more through the loud-hailer. 'We were wondering what you were doing at Christmas?'

'Who wants to know?' she demanded.

'Just about everybody,' I replied.

A blaze of gunfire told me my mother was in no mood for quips. Nonetheless, as the noise faded away, she offered what seemed like an olive branch.

'You can come in for a few minutes,' she announced. 'But make sure there's no funny business.'

An instant later she'd withdrawn the gun and vanished from sight.

'I'm going in,' I called back to the police chief. 'Wish me luck.'

'You'll need it,' came his answer as I headed for the front door. To my surprise it was off the latch, swinging open at the lightest touch. I stepped into the gloom of the hallway and was grabbed roughly from behind. Then I was frisked for weapons before being led inside.

'Sit there,' said my mother, indicating a hard wooden chair. 'And I'll go and put the kettle on.'

I did as I was told. My seat was not comfortable, but I thought it would be unwise to comment on the fact. From the kitchen I heard reassuring domestic noises. Meanwhile, I glanced around the room I was in. It had been stripped of all but the barest necessities. On the table lay a large pile of used banknotes. I was still gazing at them when my mother came back.

'You planning on doing some wallpapering?' I enquired.

She levelled the gun at me.

'If you know what's good for you, you'll cut the crap.'

'Alright,' I said. 'Sorry.'

'Now what's all this about Christmas?'

'The thing is,' I answered. 'We thought you might like to come to us this year.'

'Why should I?'

'Because you deserve a break.'

'I don't know why you're so concerned all of a sudden,' she said. 'You only call on me once in a blue moon.'

'And how often do you call on me?' I countered.

'As often as not,' she replied.

'Well then.'

'Well then nothing.'

Her new-found bluntness left me lost for words, and there followed an awkward hiatus in our conversation. Fortunately, I was saved by the kettle, its forlorn whistle calling away my reticent host. While she was gone I went to the window and peered through the slats of the blind. I saw immediately that the security cordon had been withdrawn by some thirty metres, which struck me as a sensible precaution. From this vantage point I could also see the full extent of my mother's scorched earth policy. When I'd crossed her garden a little earlier I'd been too preoccupied to notice the conspicuous absence of plant life. Gone were the neat flowerbeds which in previous years would have been full of biennials, recently transferred from the greenhouse. This structure now lay in ruins, while the lawn had become nothing more than a wilderness. Even the line of poplars that ran along the boundary fence had been felled, allowing a fresh breeze to blow in from the west.

When my mother returned she was bearing a fully laden tea tray.

'Oh,' I said. 'You shouldn't have bothered.'

'I know I shouldn't,' she replied. 'But you don't look as if you've been fed properly since the last time you were here.'

'Yes, well, I've been busy.'

'So have I.'

Something in her voice made me glance up, and I knew I was soon to discover what this was all about.

'Don't look so startled,' she said. 'I've done nothing illegal.'

'What is it then?' I asked.

She smiled. 'Remember when you said I ought to get out more?'

'Yes?'

'Well, I've been getting out more. A lot more.'

'That's good.'

'And I've realised I've been letting life pass me by for far too long. I saw that all the niceties and the considerate deeds had come to nothing, so I decided to make a few changes. First I went to the bank and took out all my money. There it is on the table. They didn't like giving it back, but they had no choice. Then I closed my accounts at the butcher's, the hairdresser's, and the garden centre. Not much, I know, but it's turned me into a free woman. I owe nobody nothing, and I can do whatever I like, whenever I like.'

'And the gun?'

'The gun's only for ornamental purposes.'

'So it's a replica, is it?'

'No,' she said. 'It's real.'

★

I ate my sandwiches and drank my tea. Then I nodded towards the street outside. 'Looks as if you've been attracting attention. Maybe you need to cool it a little bit.'

'I know, I know,' my mother conceded. 'The Feds haven't got used to me yet, so they tend to drop by from time to time. After a couple of hours they usually lose interest and disperse.' She went to the window and looked out. 'They've stuck around a little longer than usual this evening, but they'll be gone by midnight.'

'And then you'll go to bed, will you?'

'Maybe,' she answered. 'Or then again I might go out on patrol.'

I took a deep breath.

'OK,' I said at length. 'If that's what you want to do it's fine by me. I'll try to call round more often. And the invitation for Christmas still stands, of course.'

My mother thought for a moment. 'Tell you what,' she said. 'You can come here this year if you like.'

'Thanks,' I replied. 'If you're sure it won't be too much trouble.'

'I'm quite sure.'

'Alright then.'

I buttoned my coat and prepared to leave.

'Just one thing though,' she added. 'You'll have to bring your own tree.'

The Good Cop

The first time he came into the room I thought he had a rather preoccupied look about him. It was as if his mind was fully engaged in trying to solve some formidable problem, one that had been imposed on him by powers beyond his control. He paid no attention to me, although I was the only person present, and instead paced around the floor, moving from one corner to the next, until eventually he arrived back at the door. This he opened, glancing briefly outside before closing it again.

'Alright,' he said, finally breaking his silence. 'I've only got a few minutes, but if we're quick we should be able to get all this settled before he comes back.'

'Before who comes back?' I asked.

Only then did he look directly into my face. I saw that he was a tired, pale man, obviously overworked, wearing a shirt and tie (no jacket), his blue eyes regarding me through a pair of heavy spectacles. He remained standing for several long moments, then settled down in the chair opposite mine, at the other side of the desk. After removing his glasses, he leant forward and rested his head in his hands.

'You're not going to be difficult, are you?' he sighed.

I said nothing.

'Because if you're going to be difficult it makes things very difficult for me.' He raised his eyes to meet mine. Without his glasses they seemed weak, and gave him a sad, vulnerable appearance. 'I only came in here to see if I could help matters along, but if you're going to be difficult there's very little I can do. Don't you understand it would all be so much easier if you let me help?'

He continued gazing across at me, his whole face appealing for me to accept his offer.

'Well,' I said. 'What is it you want to do exactly? To help.'

His look brightened. 'I want you to trust me.'

'Why?' I enquired.

After a short pause he replaced his glasses and smiled. 'Because I'm your friend.'

★

The second time he came into the room he winced when the door clicked shut, as if the sharp sound was an intrusion, jarring the senses unnecessarily. Then he crept to the chair opposite mine and sat down, quiet as a mouse.

'Shouts a lot, doesn't he?' he ventured.

I was about to ask, 'Who does?' when he put his finger to his lips and frowned.

'It's alright,' he said. 'There won't be any shouting while I'm here, you can rely on that. Your ears can enjoy a well-earned rest. We'll have a nice gentle talk, just the two of us, and you can tell me all about it.'

I shrugged. 'There isn't much to tell.'

This brought another smile to his face, a broad, open smile of kindness and understanding. 'Yes, I suppose that's how it must seem from where you're sitting. A barrage of questions, questions, and more questions until eventually you feel as if there's nothing left to say. But let me ask you something. Have I asked you any questions?'

'None to speak of, no.'

He held out his hands, palms upwards. 'Well then. Not once have I shouted at you, or criticised you, or demanded to know anything. Like I said before, I simply want you to trust me, to think of me as your friend.' He reached into his pocket and produced a bar of chocolate, which he passed across the desk. 'Here you are. Expect you could do with a bite to eat, couldn't you?'

'Yes, thanks,' I said, unwrapping the chocolate and breaking off a chunk. 'I have been here rather a long time.'

'Three or four hours?'

'At least.'

'That is a long time,' he agreed, puffing his cheeks out. 'Yes, the waiting must be the worst part. The interminable waiting. Never knowing what's going to happen, and always wondering who'll be the next person to come through that door.'

'I hadn't thought of it like that,' I said. 'To tell the truth.'

'Really?' he asked.

'Really,' I replied.

'Well, I'm sure you will very soon.' He stood up and glanced at his watch. 'Look, I've got to go now, but I'll be back shortly, I promise. In the meantime I'd keep that chocolate hidden if I were you.'

★

The third time he came into the room he looked deeply troubled. He was carrying a steaming hot towel which he tossed to me before going over to the wall and leaning on one elbow, eyes closed, his fingers pressed hard against his brow. He maintained this stance for well over a minute. Meanwhile, I made full use of the towel, running it over my face and head, and breathing deeply as the vapours entered my pores. When at last he spoke, his voice was grave.

'I'm dreadfully sorry about this, dreadfully, dreadfully sorry. That man can be such a beast at times. A monster. Nonetheless, you must understand that he's only doing his . . .'

All of a sudden he broke off, and I looked up to see that he was staring at me with a startled expression on his face. He came forward and gave me a closer look, then slumped down in the chair opposite mine.

'Are you alright?' he asked.

'Never better.'

'Not feeling rough?'

'No, not at all.'

'Well then you'd better let me have the towel back. I'm afraid everything has to be accounted for these days. You know how things are. Nice and refreshing, was it?'

'Yes, thanks,' I replied. 'A great comfort.'

My words seemed to perk him up, because he quickly rose to his feet and walked around the room saying, 'Good, good. A great comfort. That's very good.'

Then he halted in his tracks and turned to face me again. 'The trouble is that it's likely to get worse.'

'Is it?'

'Oh, yes, much, much worse. And of course there'll be little I can do about it because I won't be here to speak up for you.'

'But I thought you said you were going to help.'

'Well . . . yes,' he stammered. 'I am going to help you, yes I am. But I can only do that . . .'

'When you come back,' I interrupted.

'Er . . . yes, that's quite right. I can only help you when I come back.'

★

The fourth time he entered the room he was sweating profusely. His shirt was unbuttoned at the collar and his tie had come loose. Under his arm he carried a sheaf of papers, which he hurriedly laid out on the desk, glancing at me from time to time and adjusting his glasses when they slipped down his nose.

'Dear oh dear,' he said, breathing heavily. 'Looks like we have an administrative problem. Can you remember what time you were brought in?'

'I wasn't brought in,' I replied. 'I came of my own accord.'

'What!' he said, plainly taken aback. 'Whatever possessed you to do such a thing?'

'I thought it was the best course of action under the circumstances.'

He put his hand to his head and began pacing round in an agitated manner.

'Have you any idea what goes on here?' he demanded. 'In this very room?'

'Well,' I answered. 'Nothing most of the time, from what I've seen.'

'Nothing!? Nothing!? How can you say that after what you've been through? Hour after hour of inter-rogation, verbal abuse and the ever-present threat of physical violence, and you call that nothing!'

'But there's only been you here,' I said. 'And you were kind enough to give me a bar of chocolate.'

He stood stock still, stared at me for several seconds, then marched out of the room.

★

When he came back I noticed he had changed his shirt. The new one was ironed, crisp and white, and his tie was knotted perfectly at the centre of his collar. He was also wearing a stiffly pressed jacket.

'Sorry about all that earlier,' he said, taking the seat opposite mine. 'Staff shortages.'

'Thought so,' I said. 'You're the good cop, aren't you?'

To my surprise he reached over and slapped me hard across the face.

'Silence!' he barked. 'We will ask the questions!'

Screwtop Thompson

SCREWTOP THOMPSON! it said on the box. HIS HEAD SCREWS RIGHT OFF! The price was two shillings and sixpence. Screwtop Thompson made his appearance in the toy shop window a few weeks before Christmas, and caught everybody's attention with his jolly laughing face. He came in several different guises. You could buy Screwtop Thompson as a policeman, a fireman, a sailor, a footballer, a boxer or a schoolmaster, each with the same expression. The policeman brandished a truncheon, the fireman held the end of a hose, while the schoolmaster wore a mortarboard and gown.

Screwtop Thompson was plump and round with a big red mouth and shiny black eyes. His head screwed off, apparently so that you could put things inside him – small coins, for example, or maybe your collection of coloured marbles. We were living in an age of austerity, so my parents agreed that Screwtop Thompson would make an ideal Christmas gift for me. I chose the fireman. The price, as I said, was two and six, or half a crown as we called it in those days.

My brother's equivalent present was a robot. It did nothing apart from march along the floor with yellow lights flashing where its ears should be, but at the time it was considered a technological marvel by children and adults alike. There were four sizes in the range, and my brother was to receive the third largest. After the two of us had made our choices, we were supposed to forget we'd ever been in the shop, so that we could be appropriately surprised when we were given our presents on Christmas Day. We did our best but it was difficult. Everybody at school was talking about the new robots and the Screwtop Thompsons, as well as all the other treasures that were arriving in the toy shop day after day. Some of them sounded fantastic.

When I heard about the car-racing kits and the 'genuine walkie-talkies' that were now becoming available, I began to wonder if I'd made the right choice with my Screwtop Thompson. At the same time, I knew it was too late to change my mind.

At last the big day came. On Christmas morning I unwrapped my present and found I had received not a fireman but a schoolmaster. It seemed that there had been such a rush for Screwtop Thompsons in the days preceding Christmas that the shop had run out of all the other lines. I hid my disappointment and reminded myself that even the schoolmaster would have the same jolly face as the rest.

When I removed the lid of the box, however, I discovered that Screwtop Thompson's head was missing. All I had was his body, wrapped in the flowing black gown. This provided a bona fide excuse for tears, and my father had to console me by saying that immediately after the Christmas holiday he would write to the manufacturer to demand an explanation, as well as a replacement head.

'We'll have to wait a couple of weeks, though,' he remarked. 'Otherwise the letter will be sure to get lost in the post.'

I stood my Screwtop Thompson on the window sill and managed to amuse myself with the rest of my gifts. Some of these were edible, of course, and included toffee and chocolate, as well as a number of little sugar mice.

As Christmas Day quickly passed, the batteries in my brother's robot began to run down, so that by teatime it would only move at half speed. Early on he'd discovered that it was altogether hopeless across carpets, and could be used only on a flat, smooth surface such as the hall floor. My mother was worried because our hallway was draughty and the weather was turning cold, and I think she was probably quite relieved when, finally, the batteries went completely dead.

As darkness fell, we forgot about toys and instead chose to watch television, the magic of Christmas flashing for hour after hour across a pale-blue screen. Then we went to bed, hoping for all our worth that it would snow overnight.

It was traditional for our cousin Martin to come to stay with us between Christmas and New Year. This was the only time we ever saw him, so we had to renew our acquaintanceship annually. At the beginning of such visits the three of us got on very well together, but relations quite often became strained as the days passed. My mother said that this was because Martin had no brothers and sisters, and was more used to playing on his own than we were. My brother and I therefore received instructions to be nice to him and to make allowances.

There had been no snow as yet, but on the day that Martin arrived the sky had turned very cold and grey, offering prospects of sledging and snowball fights. My brother and I were pleased to find that Martin shared our enthusiasm for these pursuits, and the three of us were soon planning to build an igloo.

In the meantime, we had to exchange gifts. We gave Martin solitaire, and he gave us snakes-and-ladders (which we already had). This meant that sometime after the holidays we would have to write to Martin's parents thanking them and hoping our cousin had got home safely. It also meant we would have to play snakes-and-ladders several times during the next few days. It was while preparations were being made for just such a game that I noticed one of my sugar mice had gone missing.

I'd placed all my presents on one side of the Christmas tree, separate from my brother's, with the sugar mice on top. When I discovered the loss I naturally blamed my brother and a small tussle ensued, during which he denied taking anything. Finally, my father intervened and told me I had probably lost count of how many sugar mice I'd already eaten. This seemed unlikely to me as I had previously divided them into pinks and whites and knew exactly how many there were of each. Nonetheless, my father commanded me, firmly, to drop the matter.

As all this was going on, Martin sat quietly at the table setting up the board for snakes-and-ladders. Meanwhile, my headless Screwtop Thompson stood unnoticed and forgotten on the window sill.

My brother and I had a neighbour called Conker, who often called round whether he was invited or not. He lived close by and was about the same age as me, although a good deal larger than any of my other friends. Conker was a rather rough-and-ready companion, and we were more likely to get into trouble if he was with us. He also tended to use his size to administer justice.

I remember one occasion when he saw me shove my brother into a hedge during a squabble about blackberries. A moment later, he had knocked me to the ground, and he spent the next few minutes sitting on my head singing, 'I will make you fishers of men!' at the top of his voice. As I said, a rather rough-and-ready companion. All the same, we were quite pleased to see him when he turned up one cold morning a couple of days after Martin's arrival.

Martin and Conker had met the year before, and soon we were all talking about our Christmas presents.

Conker had also received a Screwtop Thompson. His first choice had been the footballer and, lucky for him, his wish had been granted. The subject of conversation then came round to my own headless version, which Martin suddenly found a source of great amusement. With my brother and Conker as an audience, he took huge delight in mocking me for receiving a model of a schoolmaster for a Christmas present, especially one without a head!

He went on to say that he thought all the Screwtop Thompsons were stupid and babyish anyway. I pointed out that they were good for saving up in. Martin said saving up was stupid as well. Conker said this was because Martin's parents probably bought him everything he wanted, so he didn't need to save up. Martin repeated his assertion that Screwtop Thompsons were stupid.

'No, they're not!' I cried, going to the window sill to get mine. At the same instant we all saw that it was now snowing heavily outside. The argument was forgotten as we rushed about putting on our coats and boots.

My mother appeared and reminded us we needed our bobble hats as well, then the four of us spent the next few hours tumbling around in the growing whiteness. It smothered everything, so that the road and the pavement became indistinguishable under the orange glow of the street lights, which seemed to remain switched on all day (although they most probably weren't).

Before we knew it, evening had come and it was time to get warmed up indoors. We said goodnight to Conker, all of us having decided that tomorrow we would build the igloo we'd talked about.

This was easier said than done. The weather the following day turned out to be cold and harsh, and it had at last stopped snowing: ideal conditions for building an igloo. Unfortunately we were unable to agree the best way to go about it. Conker wanted to make a huge pile of snow and then burrow a way inside, while I preferred the idea of building the igloo properly from snow 'blocks'.

Martin, in the meantime, seemed much more interested in giving orders than anything else. He already had my brother digging snow with a spade that was much too large for him, and he then embarked on an independent scheme to build a giant snowman. He wouldn't let any of us help him, not even my brother, which seemed a bit unfair, so we carried on with the igloo alone. By late afternoon we were starting to wonder how Eskimos could live in such small, cold places. My brother had long since lost interest in the project, and had instead begun to build a snowman of his own, right beside Martin's. Conker and I were emerging from the igloo after a shivering competition when we saw Martin shoving a stick into my brother's snowman's neck. He obviously thought we weren't looking, and didn't seem to care that my brother was standing nearby with a very distraught expression on his face. Martin pushed the stick further and further before levering it back, so that the head was prised off and rolled onto the ground. My brother rushed forward to save his creation, but Martin knocked him to one side. This was too much for Conker, who charged from the igloo towards Martin's snowman, with the obvious intention of destroying it.

At that moment Conker's father appeared at the gate and ordered his son to come home for tea immediately. 'We've been calling you for ten minutes!' he announced, clipping the boy round the ear for good measure.

As we headed back towards our house, my brother in tears and Martin grinning quietly to himself, I noticed Screwtop Thompson, the headless schoolmaster, standing silhouetted in the window, as though he'd been observing the afternoon's events unfold.

The day before New Year was a quiet one. My parents had many things to do, they said, so they were leaving us to our own devices for a couple of hours. We were ordered not to traipse snow into the house if we went outside, and not to help ourselves to cake. Would it be alright for Conker to come round? we asked. Yes, they said, that would be alright. They would be back at teatime.

The snow had by now lost its charm for us, so instead we opted to stay indoors for the day. Martin suggested a game of snakes-and-ladders, to which my brother and I both agreed, and when Conker arrived he offered to make up a foursome. Before play could begin, however, there was a matter to settle. As Martin reached for the dice, Conker knocked him down and pinned him to the floor. Then my brother and I did our very best to screw his head right off.

They Drive by Night

It was a dark and stormy night, with the threat of rain moving rapidly in from the west. I glanced along the road, hoping that at any moment a pair of suitable headlights would appear.

Two minutes passed.

Nothing.

There were very few cars on the road this evening, and I hadn't set eyes on a van since about half past seven. The occasional vehicles that did go by all seemed to be making local journeys only. They rumbled past in a stately way, their drivers glancing casually at the lone figure standing by the roadside, and then disappeared into the gloom.

'Come on,' I murmured to myself. This was the worst day's thumbing I'd had for a long while, and it was beginning to get to me. Normally such a trip would take five or six hours at the most, yet on this occasion I'd been on the move since early morning and still had over a hundred miles to go. If I didn't get a ride very soon I was going to be stuck here for the night. And it was about to start raining.

A gust of wind tore through a clump of nearby trees and rushed across the fields pursuing a flurry of late-autumn leaves. Then, as it faded away, I heard another sound: a faint roar in the distance like a great beast labouring under an enormous burden. My ears pricked up, and a moment later a bloom of artificial light appeared between the converging hedgerows. A lorry was coming!

There were no street lamps here, so I'd positioned myself near to some reflective posts at the beginning of a lay-by. Hopefully this would help the driver spot me in good time, and give him plenty of opportunity to pull over. As the vehicle approached I saw that it was an eight-wheeler, its load hidden beneath a great tarpaulin and roped down on all sides. I stuck out my thumb.

A whistle of air brakes told me he was stopping, so I shouldered my bag and watched as the lorry veered into the lay-by and came to a noisy halt. Then I ran quickly up to the cab door on the passenger side, where a window was being wound down. A man's head emerged. He was wearing a woolly hat.

'Want a lift?' he yelled. He had to yell because of the racket the lorry was making. The whole cab seemed to be shaking with the motion of the engine, which clamoured incessantly beneath the rattling bonnet.

'Yes please!' I yelled back. 'How far are you . . . ?'

'Eh?' interrupted the man, thrusting his head even further out of the window.

'Going south?' I tried.

'South?'

I nodded and his head disappeared. Then the door swung open and I climbed up. To my surprise the man turned out to be not the driver but the driver's mate, an occupation I thought had disappeared decades before. He leant back and with some difficulty I squeezed past him into the middle seat.

The driver sat behind the wheel grinning across at me. He, too, wore a woolly hat.

'Thanks!' I shouted to him above the din. It was just as noisy inside the cab as outside, or if anything even noisier.

'You in alright?' he bellowed, jamming the lorry into gear. This involved moving my right knee out of the way, since it was pressed up against the gear stick. I complied and we pulled away just as some large drops of rain began to fall on the windscreen. Second gear required another knee movement, as did third, and not until we got into fourth was I able to relax my leg. The catseyes lit up on the road ahead, and I sat back in my seat thankful to be moving once more.

The noise made by the engine had now built up into a steady drone, augmented by the roar from the exhaust stack, which seemed to be mounted somewhere close behind us. Because of all this din I expected conversation within the cab to be kept to a minimum, but after a short while I realised that the driver was speaking to me. I strained to hear him, but only caught the end of his sentence, which sounded something like, 'Ease parts then?'

'Just passing through really!' I replied. 'I'm on my . . .'

'You what?' he said, cutting me off. His ears were hidden beneath his woolly hat.

I raised my voice. 'I said I'm on my way home for a few weeks!'

'Eh?' said the man on my left, inclining his head towards me. For the last few moments he'd sat quietly gazing through the windscreen, but now his reverie had been disturbed and he peered at me in an enquiring way.

'I was just telling your friend I'm on my way home for a few weeks!'

A look of puzzlement crossed his face as he deciphered the words. Then he nodded vigorously. 'Chance would be a fine thing!'

'You what?' said the driver, leaning across.

'He says a chance would be a fine thing!' I explained.

'Oh yes!' he agreed, after giving the remark some thought. 'Yes, indeed it would!'

The rain was coming down heavily now. It drummed on the roof and did battle with a pair of very ill-matched windscreen wipers which had been switched on shortly after I came aboard. Each wiper had its own very distinct mode of operation. The one on the passenger side swished from left to right with short, violent flicks, while the other scraped irregularly back and forth in long, languid movements that only served to move the rainwater around, rather than actually get rid of it. In consequence the driver had a broad but rather dim view of the road while his mate could see clearly but only through a very narrow segment. It occurred to me that between them their field of vision was probably quite adequate, and I wondered in an idle way if this was the reason they operated as a pair.

Certainly they had all the makings of a 'team'. For a start, the two of them were of very similar appearance, both wearing a donkey jacket as well as the woolly hat I mentioned before. They each had curly hair and thick bushy sideboards, and identical accents which placed them from the north-west, though I couldn't say exactly where. Both driver and mate seemed equally bent on pressing forward with the journey despite such atrocious weather conditions, their shared concentration evident as they stared intently at the road ahead.

When it came to verbal communication, however, there was a problem. The inside of that cab was one of the loudest places I'd ever been, yet my two companions continually tried to discuss our progress, exchanging comments on every bend, puddle or similar hazard that we encountered. This would have been alright if either had been prepared to listen to what his partner was saying. Instead, the pair of them

constantly interrupted one another with shouts of
'Eh?' or 'You what?'

At one point we passed a sign warning of a particularly steep hill approaching, and the driver began the
process of selecting low gear, a noisy operation that
entailed much revving of the engine and stamping on
the clutch pedal. While I deftly adjusted the position
of my knee in relation to the gear stick, his mate chose
the moment to make a remark about the weather.

'Looks like this rain's . . . !'

'You what?' yelled the driver.

'I said it looks like this rain's setting in for the
night!'

From my place in the middle seat I could only just
hear what was said. Therefore I suspected the driver
had picked up nothing at all. Nonetheless I could see
that he was about to attempt a reply, so I did my best
to lean back out of the way.

'What's getting in?' he shouted across me.

'Eh?' replied his mate.

'You said something was getting in!'

'Yes!' came the reply. 'For the whole night, I
shouldn't wonder!'

They both glanced towards me, apparently to seek
my opinion on the matter, so I gave a judgemental

nod of agreement and the pair of them appeared quite satisfied.

Most of the time we had this road completely to ourselves. Occasionally, however, a blurred set of lights would struggle past going the other way, indicating that we weren't the only people trying to travel in such dreadful weather. The rainwater was now practically bouncing off the tarmac, with great surges of spray being thrown up by our wheels as we ploughed southwards through the darkness.

After another mile or so a movement ahead and to the left caught my eye. Twirling round and round in the wind was a revolving sign that marked the entrance to a transport café. On top of it was a metal flap bearing a single word: CLOSED. Next moment we'd passed it by, and as the deserted roadhouse disappeared behind us I realised I hadn't eaten for hours. I'd managed to buy a box of individual fruit pies and a carton of milk round about four o'clock, but since then I'd had to concentrate so hard on getting a ride that I'd completely forgotten about food. Now my hunger was returning with a vengeance, and I felt a rush of disappointment as it dawned on me that all the cafés were more than likely shut for the night.

Fortunately my two companions were more familiar with this road than I was, and the CLOSED sign triggered off a conversation between them about when and where we were going to stop and eat. This was carried out in the normal way, with many interruptions of 'You what?' and 'Eh?' but stuck as I was between them I was able to learn quite a lot about our prospects for getting a good meal, or 'bait' as they called it.

Apparently there was a choice of two places. The first was an establishment known as The Tiger Lily, which, despite its name, had no connection whatsoever with China or Chinese cuisine. This came as a relief as my appetite was veering strongly towards steak-and-kidney pie and chips, rather than noodles. The Tiger Lily, it seemed, was renowned amongst lorry drivers (and their mates) as being *the* place to get a meal quick and cheap at any time of night. It never closed, which was presumably the reason its proprietor Charlie never had time to shave, bath or even wash. My two comrades spent a considerable amount of time exchanging jokes about Charlie's bodily hygiene. All the same they felt a certain bond of loyalty towards the man because they'd known him since before 'the accident'. What exactly had happened wasn't clear, but as I sat listening I began to form a picture of a one-armed (or perhaps one-legged) cook attempting to manage an all-night café single-handedly while wearing a heavily-stained apron. Privately I hoped that The Tiger Lily would not be our next port of call.

The alternative, I soon discovered, was a commercial restaurant called Joy's, run by a woman of the same name. This Joy apparently served up the most delicious meals imaginable, in the cleanest possible conditions, but from what I could gather ruled her customers with a rod of iron. Most of the lorry drivers on this route were actually *afraid* of her. Not only did she make them wipe their feet as they came in the door, but she forbade anyone from buttering their bread on the table rather than the plate, or from stirring sugar into their tea with the wrong utensil. She was a former beauty who'd had several husbands, all of whom were known personally to my two friends, but all of whom were now dead.

'Very harsh woman!' concluded the driver at the end of a long debate. Then he remembered that Joy's was always closed on Thursday nights when she attended her Highland Dancing Club.

'It'll have to be The Tiger Lily!' he announced.

After another twenty miles or so a glowing light appeared at the roadside, and a moment later we were turning in. As the lorry's engine fell silent it struck me that these two men would at last be able to hold a conversation without each having to yell at the top of his voice.

Yet ten minutes later, as they both sat munching their pies, mushrooms, chips and peas, neither of them uttered a single word.

Half as Nice

Auntie Pat had enjoyed a rich and colourful past, although she probably hadn't enjoyed it quite as much as she should have. Nowadays she preferred the trappings of an 'ordinary' existence. Accordingly, when she popped in for a cup of tea she seemed just like a normal auntie: she was pleasant, humorous and without fail considered the needs of others before her own. True, she was very attractive and shapely. Even as youngsters we could see that. Yet nobody would have guessed that she had once been famous. During the liberated decade she was a member of the pioneering all-girl vocal group, The Katkins, who'd had four top-twenty hits in a row. Following that she'd gone on to be one of the most in-demand session singers in the country, appearing on numerous well-known recordings. In other words, Auntie Pat had tasted stardom. In recent years, life had become much quieter.

She wasn't our real auntie, by the way. She just happened to live nearby, and Auntie Pat was what we'd always called her. Born Patricia Elspeth Stephens, she was known throughout the world of pop music by her stage name, 'Peeps' (later changed temporarily to 'Peppy'). Sometimes she'd come round while we were watching *Top of the Pops*, and occasionally they would show old black-and-white clips from years gone by. Suddenly, smiling for the cameras, would be a youthful Auntie Pat with her co-performers, instantly recognisable by their trademark 'pile it high' hairstyles. Also the shortest skirts imaginable. Their hits all used the same template: songs about loneliness that you could dance to. They also shared a common theme. Their first disc was 'BABY, COME RUNNING BACK TO ME', a minor triumph which only just scraped into the chart at number nineteen. It was enough to attract the public's attention, however, and they quickly followed up with 'BABY, COME BACK SOON'. This did much better, as did the seminal 'HOW LONG, BABY, HOW LONG?'.

There then ensued some dissent within the group as they began to squabble about the musical direction they were taking. It was the usual problem: one of the girls (not Auntie Pat) wanted to be recognised as leader of the outfit, rather than as merely one third of a trio. Only after several months had passed did they release 'HE CAME AND WENT'. It got as high as number twelve and paid the bills, but the end was now clearly in sight. As soon as the song dropped out of the charts the group split up; they'd missed the chance to record the album which might have saved them from obscurity.

The four singles had all been produced by Auntie Pat's former husband, the legendary Michael 'Dwight' Gardner, whom she married very young. Theirs was a stormy relationship, due mainly to Dwight's unpredictable nature. He had a very chequered history, to say the least, and was reputed to have made and lost his fortune several times over. Convicted for armed robbery whilst still a teenager, Dwight studied electronics in jail and at the end of his sentence found employment as a sound engineer with a record company. Very quickly he moved into production, scoring some success, and subsequently crowning himself 'the high priest of rhythm'. He also fancied himself as a vocalist, and it was his jealousy of Auntie Pat's sublime tones that ultimately soured their marriage. He had proposed to her not long after The Katkins drifted into his sphere of influence, and in the beginning they had been happy. After the group's demise, however, his attentions seemed to focus elsewhere. She left him when he began beating her up regularly.

Unfortunately, that was not the end of their entanglement with one another. Some months later Dwight unearthed a demo he had recorded as a duet with Auntie Pat, a soulful ballad entitled 'THIS AIN'T HOW IT SEEMS (IT'S A SHAME)'. The song had been written by Dwight and then shelved, apparently forgotten. Such was the way of the music industry. Now, though, Dwight decided to bring his considerable production skills into play. Working late at night in his private studio, he adapted the recording by using an editing device which crudely 'bleeped out' selected words from the song, consequently leaving much to the imagination. The remastered version was then given a new title: 'THIS AIN'T PAINT ON MY JEANS (IT'S A STAIN)', with the performance credited to 'Dwight and Peppy Gardner'.

Dwight knew a lot of people in the music business, and the tape was soon circulating amongst those 'in the know'. Once the required 'buzz' had started, an easy ride lay ahead. 'THIS AIN'T PAINT' was released as a single just before the start of the school summer holidays (a popular time for such questionable offerings) and was a massive hit, reaching number two in the charts despite being banned by all the mainstream radio stations for its presumed lewd content. Building on his own notoriety, Dwight fuelled the controversy further by holding a press conference; wearing his customary dark glasses he then sat in silence before the assembled journalists, steadfastly refusing to answer any of their questions. The stunt was just part of a perfectly timed marketing campaign aimed at milking the song for all it was worth (a rumour later emerged that the so-called 'ban' had been concocted with the help of certain radio insiders). Finally, as a *coup de maître*, the record was 'rush released' in its original unadulterated form, and Dwight made even more money. Needless to say, Auntie Pat never received a penny, though she did at last obtain her long-sought divorce. Naturally, she was mortified by the entire episode, as she disliked any kind of smut or innuendo. Therefore, she felt compelled to disappear for a while from the public's gaze.

★

Dwight later tried his hand in management, taking on an experimental rock group called The Seas of Saragossa. They quickly came to rue the day they signed their contract with him. Though they lived an apparent life of ease in a stately mansion (rented for the purpose by Dwight) they were, in fact, his virtual slaves. Instead of royalties they were paid a weekly wage, and when they ate they dined on eggs and chips in a very un-hip transport café, where they were forced to endure taunts about their long hair from the rest of the clientele. Nonetheless, Dwight worked hard on their psychedelic image. Prior to a gig one night, he arranged for there to be several photographers from the tabloid press in the audience; he then ordered the group to smash up their instruments and amplifiers 'live on stage'. Disastrously, they misunderstood his instructions, and proceeded to destroy their equipment at the end of the *very first* number. For years to come, witnesses told the story of how Dwight was seen fighting his way through from the back of the crowd shouting, 'Not yet, you idiots!' By the time he reached them it was too late. The damage was done, and he was obliged to deduct the costs from their wages.

The hapless group eventually succeeded in escaping Dwight's clutches by issuing a declaration in which they publicly eschewed all drugs. Dwight, of course, sacked them immediately without so much as a second thought. (The statement finished their careers anyway: album sales nose-dived overnight, never to recover.)

The Katkins, meanwhile, had long-since faded into oblivion. All that remained were their records (and a few clips of black-and-white film).

I had a vintage copy of 'BABY, COME RUNNING BACK TO ME' on the original label. Occasionally, I removed it from its paper jacket and gave it a spin.

Listening to it after all those years made it sound very distant and remote: I simply could not imagine that one of those faraway voices belonged to our Auntie Pat. Furthermore, I noticed that there was more to the composition than first it seemed. If you listened to it properly you came to realise that the song was full of sadness; and also a yearning for something better. Yet in reality nobody did listen properly: when the record came out, the people who bought it just wanted to dance.

This did not matter to Auntie Pat. Luckily, she was able to pursue her natural vocation as a very gifted singer for many years. Every popular group, or 'band', as they now called themselves, demanded her presence at their recording sessions. She appeared on dozens of albums, mainly as a backing singer, but also when the drink-sodden lead singer was unable to reach the required high notes, especially if 'rising fifths' were involved.

Gradually the liberated decade gave way to the progressive one; then came the more sensitive decades.

At the turn of the century a young and up-coming band put together a very sympathetic cover of 'THIS AIN'T HOW IT SEEMS'. The sleeve notes included a dedication to Auntie Pat, and their delicate approach appeared to assuage some of the pain she'd previously associated with the song. When they requested her to perform it with them at a festival, however, she gracefully declined the offer.

Auntie Pat was increasingly seeking the quiet life. She had made enough money from the session work to live on (carefully) for the rest of her days, and she no longer felt the need to sing her heart out. I couldn't help thinking, though, that she retained a vast reserve of talent as yet untapped.

Clearly others thought so too. One day the phone rang. 'Oh, hello,' said a man's voice. 'I'm trying to get in touch with a Mrs Patricia Gardner, or you may actually know her as Patricia Stephens . . . Oh, yes, that's right, Peeps. Yes, well, I wonder if you could tell her Michael rang?'

Vacant Possession

The room we chose was at the corner of the house on the first floor. We arrived mid-afternoon and found it empty: no furniture, no carpet, nothing. It was just an empty room in an empty house, but it would do for our purposes. After all, we only needed a place to sleep.

'This'll do,' said Noz, as we lugged our gear along the landing. We went inside and were soon setting up camp beds and unpacking bags.

'Nice and sunny,' I remarked. The afternoon light was streaming through the windows, giving the room a very bright and airy feel. Yes, we agreed, we should be quite at home here.

We didn't usually stay in large country houses, of course. Generally we had to find accommodation in a local bed and breakfast or commercial hotel. On this occasion, however, the owner had said that it would be alright for the 'workmen' to stay on the premises for the duration of the job. The kind offer had been passed via the land agent to the contractor, who in turn had informed us. Noz and I were sub-contractors. We were here to install a cattle grid at the front entrance to the property. The work was estimated to take about three days, so we made ourselves as comfortable as we could.

Further along the landing we found a small flight of steps leading up to the bathroom. A little further still were the backstairs going down to the kitchen. This was all we needed to know about the house. Other doors led to other rooms but we didn't even bother to look inside. We had no idea who the owner was or where he lived, nor did we care. There was a job to do and then we could go home. That was that.

After we'd settled in we had a stroll down to the front gate and did a bit of work just to say we'd got started. To tell the truth we hardly did anything more than take a few measurements and check that all the required materials had been delivered. Nonetheless, we felt better for doing it, and wandered back at dusk feeling fairly content with the world. We enjoyed our job, Noz and me, and together we made quite a good team.

'Big place, isn't it?' he said, as we approached the house.

'Yeah,' I replied. 'Must be dozens of rooms.'

'Which is ours then?'

'That one on the corner, I think. Can't really tell from here.'

'We should have left the light on.'

'Yeah,' I said. 'Suppose we should.'

Darkness had descended by the time we entered through the back door. I fumbled round for a switch and a moment later the kitchen was lit up like a Christmas tree. Then I filled the kettle and put it on the gas. Meanwhile Noz went up to the room for a 'stretch out', which was his name for a short sleep. Noz always liked a bit of a snooze around about teatime, even if only for a few minutes. It was something he'd done ever since I'd known him. He said it made him feel better.

I was a little surprised, then, when he returned almost immediately. I heard his feet coming back along the landing and downstairs, clomping over the bare floorboards and into the kitchen.

'That kettle not boiled yet?' he asked, raising the lid and looking inside.

'Give it a chance,' I answered. 'I've only just put it on.'

'We've got milk and sugar, have we?'

'Yes, of course we have! Look, I'll do the tea. You go and stretch out for a bit. I'll be up in a minute.'

'No, it's alright,' he said with a yawn. 'Don't think I'll bother.'

Noz leant against the sink puffing his cheeks until the water boiled. Then he watched with interest as I brewed up. Finally we made our way upstairs, carrying a mug of tea apiece, and went back to our room. There were no curtains, and when I turned the light on our reflections appeared in the window, moving around on a black starless background.

Noz sat on his camp bed, I sat on mine, and we enjoyed our first proper rest all day. We'd had to drive fifty-odd miles to do this job. Any less than that and we'd probably have gone home each night, but as I said before, we were staying here for free so we made the most of it.

In the top of my bag I had the paper from that morning. We'd heard the latest news repeated all afternoon on the van radio during the journey down, but I thought I'd have a browse anyway so I opened up and read the editorial. Two minutes later a familiar grunt told me that Noz had succumbed to his sleepiness and now lay dozing with his tea undrunk beside him. I knew he'd wake up just before it was completely cold and slurp it down without complaining, but personally I preferred my tea hot so I went down to the kitchen for a refill.

On the way I noticed that one of the landing floorboards was loose. It made a sort of rocking noise as I passed over it, and did the same when I returned with my fresh tea. Purely out of curiosity I stopped to examine the fault, prodding at the board with my toe and watching it move slowly up and down. The nails had come adrift at one end, and as I stood there I vaguely considered doing the owner a favour and re-fixing them. All I had to do was get a hammer from my bag and it would be done in no time. A moment later, however, I dismissed the thought. For some reason I'd begun to feel rather unwelcome on that landing, as though anything I did would be regarded as interfering. It was almost as if I was being watched, and for an instant I was tempted to look over my shoulder to make sure no one was there.

How stupid, I thought, how childish and supersti-tious. Of course there was no one there! To confirm this I glanced quickly behind me, and then headed back to the room to drink my tea before it went cold.

Noz came awake as I entered. 'Alright?' he asked.

'Of course I'm alright,' I said with some irritation. 'Why shouldn't I be?'

★

Next morning, after we'd done a couple of hours' work, we were sitting quietly eating our sandwiches when all of a sudden Noz said, 'Funny house that, isn't it?'

'Funny?' I asked.

'Yeah.'

'What sort of funny?'

'Well, you know, all higgledy-piggledy.'

'Oh. Yeah. Suppose it is, now you come to mention it.'

'I mean, why put the bathroom up those little stairs, and the kitchen right at the back, miles away from anywhere?'

'Well,' I replied. 'It's just the way they built places in those days. They sort of added bits on as they went along. You know, when they had the money.'

'All the same,' said Noz. 'Seems a bit funny putting the bathroom at the top of those little stairs. Stuck on its own, like.'

A long moment passed, and then I said, 'Is that why you didn't go up there last night?'

'Course not!' he exclaimed.

'Well, why didn't you then?'

'Just didn't need to, that's all.' Noz closed his sandwich box and stood up. 'Right,' he said. 'I suppose we'd better get on.'

I remained seated. 'Wait a sec, I've only had one sandwich.'

He tutted. 'How long are you going to be exactly?'

'Not long,' I said.

'Alright, well hurry up, can't you?'

This time it was Noz who sounded irritated. He was obviously a bit rattled about something, and I had a feeling I knew what it was. We resumed work shortly afterwards and there was no mention of the house, or its unusual layout, for the rest of the day. At dusk, however, when we packed in, I decided to clear the air a little. Both of us had been fairly snappy with each other all afternoon, pointing out one another's mistakes and generally not getting along together. In the end I decided to say something.

'Look, Noz,' I began. 'I think you're right about that house.'

He gave me a sharp glance. 'How do you mean?'

'Well,' I said. 'I think it's fairly creepy actually.'

'Do you?'

'Yeah. Stupid, isn't it?'

'Yeah,' he said, grinning. He looked quite relieved. 'It's because it's all empty, I suppose. Oh well, I'm glad you've mentioned it. I thought it was just me.'

'No, I'm the same.'

'That's alright then.'

'Yeah.'

While we talked we'd been walking slowly back towards the house, now once again engulfed in darkness.

'All those windows don't help,' remarked Noz. 'They're like eyes watching you.'

'What we'll have to do,' I said, 'is sort of ride it out. Make a joke about it being haunted sort of thing.'

'Alright.' Noz approached the kitchen door, opened it and switched the light on. At the same instant his eyes dilated and he let out an unearthly scream.

'I knew you'd do that,' I said, shoving him through the door.

Next thing, we had the kettle lit and I was busy washing up the mugs so we could have some tea. For all his bravado Noz nonetheless declined to go ahead for a 'stretch out' until I was ready, but eventually we both headed up to the room, talking loudly as we went.

Crossing the landing I again stepped on the loose floorboard, so that it made its usual rocking noise.

'Right,' I said, with resolution. 'Let's get this fixed for a start.'

I got a hammer and some nails from my tool bag and immediately began the repair. Meanwhile Noz scanned some of the other boards.

'This one could do with a couple of nails too,' he said. 'And here.'

We ended up spending about twenty minutes going over the whole landing, making a lot of noise with our hammers and tramping around as if we owned the place. Like most jobs we did it took longer than expected, but when we'd finished we stood looking at each other with big grins on our faces.

'That's better,' I said. 'I feel much more at home here now.'

'Yeah,' agreed Noz. 'Don't know what we were worried about really.'

We went into the room and sat down to enjoy our teas which, we soon discovered, had gone cold.

'I'll go and make some more,' announced Noz.

'Oh right,' I said. 'Shall I come with you?'

'Nah,' he said. 'Doesn't matter.'

He took the mugs and set off along the landing, whistling a shrill tune.

'Don't forget, no sugar for me!' I called as he went.

'Righto!' he replied.

I propped the door open. The whistling continued but became more distant as he descended the back-stairs. Then I listened while he clanked about in the kitchen. I heard water surging through the pipes as he filled the kettle and rinsed out the mugs. A few seconds passed. The water stopped running and the whistling ceased. Noz had fallen silent as he waited for the kettle to boil, apparently quite content to be all alone at the bottom of the stairs.

★

And as I sat in that room, watching the door and listening, it never occurred to me to look over my shoulder.

A Public Performance

By the autumn of 1970 I was coming under intense pressure to buy a coat. A military greatcoat to be precise. Everyone I knew had one (everyone in the sixth form, that is) although they were officially banned from school. To avoid being left behind I had to get one as well. There were lots to choose from. Barry, for example, had an ex-Army coat of olive green, while Mike's was blue-grey (RAF). Robert, meanwhile, favoured a huge brown overcoat that had been passed down through the Italian side of his family. It had a collar which could be turned up against the wind, and gave him the look of Giacomo Puccini in the famous photograph from 1910. The exception to the group was Phil, who always wore a US Army combat jacket. This was the other option open to me: I could either get a combat jacket or a greatcoat. The weather was turning chilly, so I decided on a coat. In that way I could both look cool and feel warm at the same time.

One quiet afternoon during half-term I caught a bus into Bristol and headed for a shop I'd noticed at the foot of Colston Hill. Looking back I suppose the army surplus store in Gloucester Road would have been a more suitable destination. They had recently extended their range of stock to cater for the increasing demand, and no doubt could have readily supplied a garment to fit my requirements. The trouble was, I knew that everybody else had bought their coats there. I didn't want to wear the same 'uniform' as the rest of them, so I made my way to Colston Hill.

The shop I had in mind was called Visual History. It specialised in military artefacts, and its window was crammed with all sorts of muskets, blunderbusses and swords. Also, displayed on a mannequin, a very impressive coat. It was tailored from a fine grey cloth, and had two rows of gold buttons up the front. There were epaulettes of burnished gold on the shoulders, and gold flashes on the cuffs. I knew the moment I saw it that this was the coat for me. It clearly originated with the Russian Imperial Army, and I guessed it had once belonged to a Cossack. This was evident because the lower part of the coat was widely flared, an obvious prerequisite for riding a horse. Without a second thought I entered the shop.

There were no other customers, but the shopkeeper ignored me when I came in, and continued reading the newspaper that was spread out across his counter.

'Afternoon,' I said.

He peered up over the rim of his glasses.

'Could I have a look at that coat in the window, please?'

An expression of curiosity now crossed the shopkeeper's face. He glanced at me, then at the coat. Then back at me again.

'You're not wasting my time, are you?' he asked.

'No, no,' I replied. 'I'm thinking of buying it.'

The curious expression disappeared and was replaced with a sort of surprised half-smile, as if the shopkeeper was remembering some good news he'd heard earlier in the day. I watched as he climbed over a panel into the window display, returning a moment later with the coat. He quickly folded away his newspaper and laid the coat before me. It was very large and heavy.

'Pre-Revolutionary Russian,' I announced, examining the epaulettes in a knowing manner.

'Oh,' said the shopkeeper. 'Is it?'

'I think so, yes.'

After a long pause he nodded gravely. 'You know, I think you're probably right.'

'Can I try it on?'

'Of course you can. There's a changing cubicle over there.'

I entered a narrow booth and took off the raincoat I'd been going round in for the past two years. It was off-white in colour, and closely resembled the one worn by Steve McQueen in *Bullitt*. But I'd had enough of it. I hung it from the hook and proceeded to put on my greatcoat for the first time.

'Odd,' I said, talking through the walls of the cubicle. 'There don't appear to be any buttonholes.'

'No, there aren't,' came the shopkeeper's muffled voice. 'The buttons are only for show.'

'How do I fasten it up then?'

'There should be some little hooks inside the front of the coat,' he said. 'And some little eyes. You have to match them up.'

With some difficulty I did up the hooks. Then, to my delight, in one of the pockets I discovered a broad belt with a big silver buckle. This left no doubt that the coat must once have belonged to a Cossack. Moreover, it seemed to fit me perfectly. I adjusted the collar and emerged from the cubicle. The shopkeeper took one look at me and laughed out loud.

'Something wrong?' I asked.

'No, no!' he cried. 'It's fantastic.'

'Have you got a mirror?'

'Afraid not,' he said, wiping tears from his eyes. 'Sorry.'

The price was two pounds and ten shillings. At that time I earned one pound ten at my Saturday job, so the coat was by no means cheap. I decided, however, that it would be a good investment for my forthcoming winters as a student at some faraway university (or, as it turned out, polytechnic).

'I'll take it,' I said, producing a hard-earned five pound note.

The shopkeeper can't have had any other customers that day because his till was completely empty. Informing me that he would have to go and get some change, he left me inside the shop, still wearing the coat, and locked the door as he went out. Half a minute later he returned, accompanied by another man who I assumed came from a neighbouring shop. The two of them stood peering in at me for some moments before quickly turning away and moving out of sight again. When he returned for a second time the shopkeeper was smiling broadly.

'Here we are,' he said, letting himself in. He gave me my change and then asked if I'd like the coat wrapped.

'No, I think I'll wear it now,' I replied. 'Looks quite cold out there.'

'Suit yourself.'

He wrapped up my raincoat instead, and when I departed he insisted on shaking my hand.

'You've made my day,' he explained.

On the journey home a strange sense of solitude came over me. I sat on the bus in my newly acquired coat feeling quite aloof from my fellow passengers. Actually I felt sorry for them as they undertook their humdrum workaday journeys, while I enjoyed the unhurried timelessness of half-term. When we came to my stop I turned my collar to the wind and disembarked.

Of course, I was not at all surprised by my brother's response on seeing the coat. He was an immature fourteen-year-old and I took no notice when he asked me where I'd hired my tent. The reaction of my mother, on the other hand, was most disappointing. As I entered the house she gave out a sort of gasp and instantly pushed a folded handkerchief to her mouth. I asked her what she thought of my coat but she was unable to answer.

'Want a cup of tea?' I enquired, reaching for the kettle. Without replying she rushed into the next room.

I was just stirring the pot when she returned. By now I'd taken the coat off and hung it up. After taking a deep breath, my mother asked me to put it on again, then she walked round and round me, looking me up and down. Finally, she undid the hooks and examined the label inside. It said:

MADE IN GREAT BRITAIN

XL

DRY CLEAN ONLY

OTHELLO THEATRICAL SUPPLIES LTD

Kindly, my mother offered to remove the label.

★

The following Tuesday evening I went to see Pink Floyd at the Colston Hall in Bristol. They were touring with their latest offering, a semi-orchestral composition entitled 'Atom Heart Mother'. I had actually attended the first ever public performance of the piece earlier that summer during the Festival of Blues and Progressive Music at the Bath & West Showground, Shepton Mallet. Along with a quarter of a million others I'd endured two days of searing heat and dust. By the time Led Zeppelin played late on the Sunday afternoon there was virtually no drinking water available, and unscrupulous vendors were charging as much as five shillings for a can of Coca-Cola. As a callow youth I had believed this drink could quench my thirst and actually paid the fee not once, but twice. Ultimately, the event would be washed out by heavy rain, but not before Pink Floyd had made their long-awaited appearance late on the Saturday night. 'Atom Heart Mother' was an ambitious instrumental piece in which the band were augmented by a full brass section from a proper orchestra, along with a ten-member choir. There was also a massive TV screen showing close-ups of all the on-stage action, plus an extended light show and a firework display during the closing notes of the finale. Yet somehow I'd managed to sleep through the whole thing, having lain down on my groundsheet while I waited for it to begin. When I awoke it was the early hours of the morning, the showground was enveloped in mist, and all was quiet. Now, several months later, I had a chance to make up the deficit. Pink Floyd were on tour again! With my ticket in my pocket I set off for the Colston Hall. The first person I saw when I entered the crowded foyer was a girl from school called Alison who I was quite friendly with. (In fact I quite fancied her and had asked her out a couple of times. She had declined the offer in a gentle, sympathetic sort of way, and we were now officially 'friends'.) She was standing with some people who'd left school the previous year, none of whom I knew very well. As I approached, wearing my belted Russian Imperial Army greatcoat, one of them looked at me, then said something to Alison and she glanced in my direction. Instantly, she put her hand over her face, closed her eyes and half-turned away. Sensing I was intruding on some private moment, I went and stood somewhere else. The first part of Pink Floyd's show included another new offering, an avant-garde composition entitled 'Alan's Psychedelic Breakfast'. This non-musical piece of work was to be found on their latest album, and the band had admitted in the music press that it was only a 'filler track' because they didn't have enough viable material. Nevertheless, a paying audience sat and watched as one of their roadies prepared his breakfast live on stage, accompanied by a 'sound-melange' of snap, crackle and pop, sizzling bacon, and, surreally, the voice of Jimmy Young. At the interval we filed out of the auditorium and into the bar for a drink. There was someone behind me giving the performance the benefit of his opinion, which was apparently at odds with that of his peers, who had roundly applauded it a few moments earlier. As a matter of fact I thought he was quite courageous, announcing as he did that he thought the whole spectacle was quite absurd, ridiculous even, and a prime example of the folly of youth. To my surprise, none of his companions seemed to disagree. They smiled at me, one by one, as they passed me by. Turning up my collar, I went and stood by the doorway.

a note on the author

Magnus Mills is the author of six novels, including *The Restraint of Beasts*, which won the McKitterick Prize and was shortlisted for both the Booker Prize and the Whitbread First Novel Award in 1999. His other novels are *The Scheme for Full Employment*, *All Quiet on the Orient Express*, *Three to See the King*, *Explorers of the New Century* and *The Maintenance of Headway*. His books have been translated into twenty languages. He lives in London.

a note on the type

The text of this book is set in Bembo. This type was first used in 1495 by the Venetian printer Aldus Manutius for Cardinal Bembo's *De Aetna*, and was cut for Manutius by Francesco Griffo. It was one of the types used by Claude Garamond (1480–1561) as a model for his Romain de l'Université, and so it was the forerunner of what became standard European type for the following two centuries. Its modern form follows the original types and was designed for Monotype in 1929.